THE MYSTERY OF THE
RUSSIAN CIRCUS SCHOOL

By Judith Marie Austin

Illustrations by Carlotta Tormey

To the Children of the World –
May They be Friends

Published by GlobalFriends Press

Copyright © 1996 by GlobalFriends$_{TM}$

All rights reserved. No part of this book
may be used or reproduced in any manner whatsoever
without written permission except in the case of
a brief quotation embodied in critical articles and reviews.

First Edition
Printed in Hong Kong through the Wyatt Group.

For more information contact:
Book Editor, GlobalFriends Press
1820 Gateway Drive, Suite 320
San Mateo, CA 94404

ISBN: #0-9638614-6-8

ONE

"Would you like something to drink?" the flight attendant asked.

Jody looked up from the letter she was reading. "Just some water, please."

"Hey, Jody!" Marissa leaned over her father's tray table and touched Jody's arm with her pen to get Jody's attention. "Are you using all the postcards you picked up at the airport?"

"I've got this one left." Jody reached in front of Marissa's father and gave the postcard to Marissa. "'S'cuse me, Mr. Rosen."

"Sure." Marissa's father smiled, glancing up from the newspaper he was reading.

"Thanks!" Marissa picked up the pen from her lap.

Jody, Marissa, and Marissa's father were flying to Moscow, Russia. Because Marissa's father had to be there on business, Marissa's GlobalFriend, Katrina, had invited them all for the annual Winter Fest. There was a possibility that they might be able to watch some of Katrina's classes at the Moscow Circus School. Because Marissa and Jody had been taking gymnastics for three years now, they might even

be allowed to participate in the classes! It was a dream come true!

"She says here that she has to take all the regular academic subjects too. Like math. Even though she goes to a circus school." Jody was reading letters that Katrina had written to Marissa. Jody was Marissa's GlobalFriend from New Mexico. She was tall for twelve and had really long, straight black hair with dark brown eyes. Warm, honest and naturally athletic, Jody was liked by everyone who knew her because she was so enthusiastic about everything.

Marissa signed her name at the bottom of her postcard and looked up again. "That's because it's like a regular school, but a whole lot more."

Marissa had offered to let Jody read Katrina's letters about the circus school and life in Russia.

Jody was reading all the letters twice. "That must be totally strange. Can you see yourself juggling one hour and doing multiplication the next?"

Marissa leaned forward again, her thick, dark blonde hair brushing her face. "Katrina wrote to me once that the motto of the school is 'The balance is better if the head is full.' She said it means if your head is full of knowledge, you'll perform better in the circus. She has to work just as hard at the regular school subjects as she does at learning circus skills."

"What kinda circus classes do they take?" Jody asked.

"Acrobatics and gymnastics." Marissa thought for a minute. "And balancing and juggling," she added.

"Don't all the kids at the school have to take ballet, too? Like you. Katrina says it gives them... How'd she put it? Oh, yeah. 'Grace and beautiful movement'." Jody was shuffling through Katrina's letters. "What does Katrina want to be?" Jody asked, still looking through letters.

"A tightrope acrobat." Marissa leaned forward. "Her sister, Alexandria, was also accepted into the school. She wants to be an animal trainer."

"What do you mean 'was accepted?' Isn't the school open to everyone?" Marissa's father asked.

Marissa shook her head, her blonde hair flying. "No! You can apply when you're eleven. But only if you have really excellent grades in sports and regular scholastic subjects. And you don't necessarily get in. The 'try-outs' last a week. And you're judged on everything! Your 'try-out' performances, your attitude, your scholastic ability, even your health records. Everything! Only one in every seventy kids who apply is accepted."

"One in seventy!" Jody was amazed.

"How long has the school been open?" Marissa's father quizzed.

Marissa scratched her head. "It was opened sometime in the 1920's, I think."

"1927," Jody said, digging through the letters again. "Here it is!" she announced triumphantly. "The original school was in a couple of old circus wagons. Then the Russian government gave them an old stable and practice ring. It was added onto several times. Then in

1971, the government built a whole new school for seven hundred students with three circus rings for classes and performances," She was reading from one of Katrina's letters.

"Are those the photos?" Marissa's father asked. "Could I see them again, please?"

Jody showed him the pictures that were taken at the Moscow Circus

School. There were photos of acrobats balancing on wires and kids doing handstands on other kid's shoulders. More children were swinging by their knees, arms outstretched, from trapeze bars. One girl was riding a unicycle across a low wire. A boy was juggling about fifteen balls and plates. Another boy was sitting on the shoulders of a man and had a rooster perched on top of his head. A group of white horses circled the circus ring. They were rearing back onto their hind feet, pawing the air.

"This is great!" he exclaimed, looking at a picture of Katrina on the low wire. "It's wonderful that you've got photos from the school!"

"That's why I joined the GlobalFriends Club." Jody looked up. "You make friends all over the whole, wide world. You get to know what's important to other kids What they like and don't like, what they do, what they want to be."

"I like all my GlobalFriends!" Marissa exclaimed. "In some ways, we're really different. Like how we dress and stuff. But most of the time, we're really the same. Especially on the inside. How we think and feel. We all want to travel the world and be somebody! Like I just know Katrina's going to be a great tightrope artist! She's going to be famous everywhere!" Marissa's brown eyes sparkled with confidence.

The flight attendant leaned over their seats. "Are your seat belts fastened?" she asked, checking. "We'll be landing in about twenty minutes. Please have your passports and visas ready."

TWO

Jody tried not to stare at the group of Russian circus students hurrying out to the performance rings. The girls were dressed in leotards and the boys in briefs. They all had on tights and thin, slipper-type shoes on their feet. The girls all had long hair pulled back in ponytails or braids. Jody yanked her attention back to Katrina.

Katrina was elegantly beautiful. Not too tall and not too short, she had long red hair fastened back in a braid and green eyes. "This is the locker area," she was saying. "The younger students in the school have lockers here and the older students have lockers on the other side of the performance arena." She opened her locker, pointing inside. "We keep our coats, hats, mittens and boots here. Also school books and sometimes..."

Katrina drew out a dazzling blue leotard covered with sparkling sequins. "Sometimes performance costumes." She spread the leotard on a bench in front of her locker. "This is the costume I will wear during our show at the Winter Fest."

"Out of over a hundred kids in her class, Katrina was chosen to be one of five to perform in the festival!" Marissa burst out, proudly.

"Wow," Jody said breathlessly.

In keeping with her serious nature, Katrina nodded solemnly. "It is a great honor. Students are never allowed to perform in public until they graduate. But this year, the Winter Fest officials wanted to have a... How do you say it in English?" She looked confused, then smiled. "A special performance of students in training. To show how they progress from the first year in school to graduation. It is more to show the school as a whole than to show any particular student. But I still get..." At a loss for English words again, she rubbed her leotard-covered stomach.

"Butterflies!" Marissa exclaimed, rubbing her stomach, too.

Jody was looking around the locker room. She noticed a boy at the far end of their row of lockers. "Is this locker room for girls and boys?" she asked, curious.

"Yes," Katrina assured. "But we dress in separate dressing rooms." She pointed to a door at the other end of the locker area. "The girl's dressing room is there." She turned around, pointing in the opposite direction. "The boy's is there. This area is just for storage lockers."

A group of construction men walked in. They were looking around and talking.

"What are they doin'?" Jody asked, staring.

"They are working on the school to add more classrooms and more dormitories. Dormitories are our sleeping rooms," Katrina explained.

"They are also working on both locker areas. And they are re-flooring the main hall to the performance arena. For a time, everyone entering and leaving the arena must go through the locker rooms. Even the animals. Yesterday, a seal hid in one of the lockers and would not come out!"

Marissa giggled, and both Jody and Katrina started to laugh.

"Come," Katrina said, still smiling. "Let me show you the performance rings."

She hung her show costume back in her locker and led the way out into the arena. It was like a theater. There were three circus rings in the center of the stage floor. Rows of audience seats curved around three sides, rising sharply toward the extremely high ceiling.

The audience seats were empty, and all three circus rings were crowded with students and instructors.

"What are they doing?" whispered Marissa.

Katrina pointed out that the students in the closest ring were practicing acrobatics. Even now, one student was standing on the shoulders of another and a third was climbing up to stand on his shoulders. "He will do a handstand on top," Katrina whispered,

13

pointing. "Look." As they watched, spellbound, the boy student positioned his hands on the shoulders of the second boy and raised his feet, straightening in the air. He didn't look like he was even twelve years old!

"How'd he do that? What if somebody had moved or...jerked. Or anything," whispered Jody, breathless.

"Trust. You must always trust who you are working with." Katrina looked serious. "Trust and timing are everything in the circus." She pointed. "Look there."

In the second ring, a girl juggled six balls in the air, each a different color, each a different size. Keeping a steady rhythm, she never missed one. "Timing is as important as trust," Katrina repeated. "Someday she may juggle flaming torches in the dark."

In the third ring, a boy directed dogs through a series of hoops. "We have no large animals at the school," Katrina informed them. "Only dogs and seals. And sometimes they bring in horses. This week is different. A traveling circus from Mogodon in Siberia has come to Moscow for the Winter Fest. All the performers and circus people are staying here at the school in our dormitories. The animals are here, too. They brought horses and elephants, lions and tigers. They are rehearsing during the evenings."

Marissa was watching the dogs. "What's he feeding them?"

"Ahhh..." Katrina searched her memory for the right word. "Treats," she said, smiling. "Animal training is taught with rewards for good behavior."

They started back toward the locker area. "Why do circuses have performing rings?" asked Marissa.

"Circuses began as horseback riding shows," Katrina explained. "A long time ago, a performer who worked with horses realized that the horse was better balanced, more level and even, if it was ridden in a circle. The size of the circle determined the speed of the horse as well."

They walked into the locker room. Katrina noticed that her locker door was still open. "Excuse me. I should close that, then we will go to the animal area." Always disciplined and careful, she stepped over to her locker, glancing inside.

Suddenly, she was pulling everything from her locker. Her coat, scarf and mittens lay on the floor. Her books and papers were scattered. "Didn't I put away my show costume?" she asked Marissa and Jody. Katrina sounded panicked. "Where is my show costume?!"

THREE

"Tilt back," Katrina instructed Jody. "Don't worry. I will catch you if you fall. Trust me. That's right. Now raise one leg. Tilt back more..."

Marissa looked on as Katrina coached Jody through a gymnastics routine.

Jody flipped over, landed with her legs split, rolled forward and rose to her feet, all in one motion.

"Wonderful! You did it perfectly!" Katrina cried. Jody smiled shyly. "Is there anything you would like to practice?" Katrina turned toward Marissa.

"Could you teach me how to do that cartwheel to a one-handed handstand to a flip?" Marissa asked. "Especially the movement between the cartwheel and the handstand. It looks so smooth when you do it. And I just don't get it."

Katrina's brow puckered. "Don't get it?" she repeated, confused.

"She means that she doesn't understand it," Jody explained, smiling.

Katrina nodded, looking relieved. "It is really quite simple. Watch." Katrina gracefully spun off into a cartwheel, then did a second cartwheel that ended in a one-handed handstand. "Did you see it?" she asked, still upside down, balancing on one hand. "You tuck..."

A group of students walked by, talking loudly. One of the girls pointed at Katrina, said something in Russian, and they all laughed.

Katrina flipped to her feet, looking self-conscious. "Perhaps I could show you another way..."

"What did they say?" Marissa was curious.

"Nothing important." Katrina brushed past it.

"But what was it?" Marissa persisted.

"Olga might have been chosen to perform in the Winter Fest if I had not been. She is still a little upset," Katrina explained.

"She's mad about it?" Jody asked.

"She's probably just jealous," announced Marissa.

Katrina held up her hands to stop them from talking about it. "I think she was just a little upset," she repeated, defending Olga.

To change the subject, Marissa asked, "Did you ever find your costume?"

"No, it is gone. I spoke with the Head Costumer, and another costume has been made for me." Looking, Katrina saw that her classmates were heading toward the locker area. "Oh, I am sorry, Marissa. Class has ended. We can study the move tomorrow."

* * *

Marissa handed Jody her sweater from their visitor's locker. "Wait 'til I get back to the hotel. I'm going to write to every one of my GlobalFriends and tell them what a great country Russia is! And what a great school this is! I'm having the most fun..." They heard a soft scream.

Racing to Katrina's locker, they saw her clothing scattered on the floor. Katrina stared at them from her open locker, her face stricken, tears in her eyes. "It is gone! My new costume is gone!"

FOUR

"Do things disappear at the school all the time?" Marissa asked. She and Jody were sitting on the bench in front of Katrina's locker. After pulling everything out, Katrina was putting all of her belongings back in order.

"Yeah," Jody added. "Did you ever have anythin' else stolen?"

Katrina hung up her coat and turned to face them. "No. Nothing is ever stolen. One of the most important teachings of the school is to trust. Someday our lives will depend on the people around us. For example, a team performance on the trapeze, handing trapeze bars to each other, swinging from person to person. We must trust other people. Or there would be no circus." She sat down on the bench beside Jody.

A man entered the locker area. He announced something in Russian. Katrina listened to what he was saying and then she stood up. "Come. We must not sit here. The elephants are going out to the performance rings now."

"Can we watch?" Jody was excited.

"Yes. But not too closely. Do not try to touch them, and do not make any sudden moves." Katrina stepped back into another aisleway between the rows of lockers. "We can watch from here."

Surrounded by six handlers, three enormous elephants lumbered single-file through the locker area. Like in a parade, the second elephant held the first elephant's tail in his trunk. The third elephant held the second elephant's tail in his trunk.

"Why are they doing that?" Marissa pointed.

"They are trained to walk that way," Katrina explained. "Elephants can be curious. They like to explore things with their trunks. This keeps their trunks out of trouble. It also keeps them together when they are being moved from place to place."

"Elephants aren't dangerous, are they?" Jody didn't understand why it was important for the elephants to stay together.

"They are not dangerous like a tiger is dangerous. They can be dangerous because they are so very large and heavy. They are not always aware of where they are stepping. Because of where their eyes are positioned, they cannot always see their feet." Katrina gestured to the nearest elephant.

"Like a horse." Jody was staring at the elephants.

"Yes, but much larger even than a horse." Katrina watched as the last elephant swayed out to the performance arena.

The three friends moved back to Katrina's locker, grouping on the bench again. "I just can't understand why your costumes keep disappearing..." Marissa started.

"Or why somebody would take 'em," Jody put in. "It's not like they could ever wear 'em. I mean, people here at the school would know they're yours."

Katrina nodded. "That is true."

"They might be taking them just to be mean," Marissa guessed. She was thinking about the girl Olga who might have been chosen to perform if it weren't for Katrina.

"Or they might be tryin' to stop you from being in the Winter Fest." Jody was thinking about Olga, too. She leaned forward on the bench, looking at Katrina. She was speaking louder than usual to be heard over the noisy construction workers who were working in the locker room. Several men were measuring lockers and doorways. They were laughing and talking.

"Or maybe the thief isn't connected with the school." Marissa was looking at the construction workers. "Maybe someone took them for his daughter. Because he thought they were pretty."

Katrina nodded slowly. "It is possible. I asked the Head Costumer to leave the costume on this bench. Perhaps someone took it who did not know that it was a show costume."

"Are you sure she brought it over?" Marissa asked.

"Yes, I saw it. I didn't mean to leave it out, but I was late for my science class, and we had a test today."

"Where was the first costume?" Jody was thinking.

"I remember that I hung it in my locker." Katrina was thinking, too.

22

"But I don't think you closed the locker door." Jody shook her head. "No, you didn't. Remember? You were givin' us a tour of the school. We came back here after seein' the performance arena. And the first thing you did was go over to your locker 'cause you left the door open!"

The same man who had announced the elephants entered the locker area. Like before, he was talking very loudly in Russian. Katrina stood up again.

"So..." she said slowly. "It is possible that someone not of the school took my costumes. But why?" She turned to take two Russian history books out of her locker. "Come, we will have to hurry." She

turned back around to see Marissa and Jody still sitting on the bench. "Oh, I am sorry," she exclaimed, smiling. "I forgot that you do not speak Russian. The man that was here... he is bringing the Mogodon tigers through. We have to leave the locker area."

The two friends leapt up, dashing for their visitor's locker three locker rows away. As they snatched clothing from the locker, Marissa yelled, "Hey, Katrina? Maybe the GlobalFriends Club can help. We've solved mysteries before!"

"That's right!" Jody cried. "Sometimes GlobalFriends from other countries have totally great ideas. It couldn't hurt to ask!"

"We will have to contact them quickly," shouted Katrina from her locker. "The Winter Fest performance is a week from today. If I am to perform, I must have a costume!"

A large heavy-set man stepped into the performance arena doorway. He was shouting and shaking his finger at Katrina. Marissa and Jody crept around the rows of lockers. "I wonder what he's saying?" whispered Marissa.

The man whirled and disappeared into the arena. Katrina looked upset. She closed her locker door quietly, turned and saw them standing in the aisleway.

"I am sorry," she said, close to tears. "We should not have been so loud. It is disturbing to the students practicing in the arena."

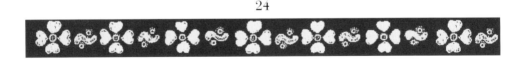

FIVE

Within sight of a beautiful onion-domed cathedral, a Moscow park was flooded in one area to make a winter skating rink. On the same side, a restaurant served hot refreshments to the skaters. Jody, Marissa and Marissa's father were all warming up with cups of hot tea. Katrina and her sister, Alexandria, were going to meet them here later.

They were watching the skaters, and some of them were very good! Jody could hardly take her eyes off them. The men were leaping into the air. Barely touching the ice, they would spin so fast it made her dizzy. It was like being a part of the Ice Capades. But it was real!

"Look at them!" Marissa nudged Jody's elbow. Gliding and twirling, a man and woman were ice dancing to the music being played over the loudspeakers in the park.

Marissa took a sip of her milky tea. "How are your meetings going, dad?" she asked her father.

"Better than I'd hoped." Marissa's father tasted his tea. His eyes were twinkling. "How's school?"

"Totally radical!" cried Jody.

"Awesome!" Marissa exclaimed.

Marissa's father laughed, looking at the two friends. "Well, I guess you can't beat two out of two."

"Mr. Rosen, you should see them practicin' on the trapeze. And they're only a couple of years older than us. I mean, they're wearin' safety wires now in case they fall, but it's the coolest thing I've ever seen! It's like flyin'!" Jody could hardly get the words out fast enough.

"I like the tightrope. And you should see Katrina on the tightrope! She has to wear a safety wire, too, of course. But she said she's only fallen once. And that was last year! She looks so sure of herself and so graceful! I wish I was that good." Marissa sighed longingly.

"The animals are so cool! I got a chance to work with the seals today, and it was radical! I've never even seen a seal up close before. Today I got to pet 'em and coax 'em through hoops and give 'em treats!" Jody leaned back in her chair. "Bein' a clown with animals would be awesome!"

Outside the window, a light snow had started to fall dusting over the skaters on the ice rink. The lights on the cathedral sparkled. The brilliant colors of the onion-shaped domes were deeper and richer in the shadowy light of the city at night.

Marissa's father leaned back in his chair, too, taking in the view. "Isn't this great?" He took another sip of tea. "So, Rissie, what do you like best?"

Marissa sighed. "Everything!"

"If you had to pick a favorite, what would it be?" he persisted, smiling.

Marissa thought about it. "Probably the group acrobatics," she said slowly, still thinking. Then she brightened. "Yeah, definitely! I like working with the other kids. And being part of a group. And knowing someone's going to catch me if I fall." She stopped suddenly.

"What's the matter?" her father asked quickly.

Marissa twisted her mouth. "Well, someone is stealing Katrina's show costumes. The costumes that she's supposed to wear for the performance at the Winter Fest."

Her father was surprised. "Stealing?"

"We think they're bein' stolen. They're missin', anyway. Two of 'em. One was taken yesterday, and the other was taken the day before." Jody poured more milk into her tea.

"Right out of her locker," explained Marissa.

"Are there locks on the lockers?" quizzed Marissa's father, concerned.

"No. Katrina said that one of the big things at the school is learning to trust. Because someday your life will depend on trusting someone. All of a sudden, it made sense to me because that's what group acrobatics is all about. Trusting the rest of the people in your group to do exactly what you expect them to do." Marissa looked serious. "Trust is really important."

Winding through the crowded restaurant, Katrina and Alexandria finally walked up to the table. Katrina's eyes were red and blurry. She had been crying. "Another costume is gone. My third costume is gone."

SIX

Katrina's sister, Alexandria, was sixteen. Tall and red-haired like Katrina, she spoke English with hardly a trace of accent. Within moments she had ordered another round of hot tea, freshly baked bread and cheeses. "Would you like to try some caviar, too?" she asked before the waiter had a chance to move away.

"What's that?" Jody was curious.

"A Russian specialty," Marissa's father answered with a grin.

Alexandria laughed merrily. "It is fish eggs. Salty fish eggs. We eat it on bread with cheese. I believe in the States you eat it on bread with sour cream and bits of onion and egg."

"No, thanks," Jody decided.

Marissa was thinking. "I'd like to try it. Just because it's different, doesn't mean it's not wonderful."

"Good for you," her father said. "Order enough for all of us. Maybe Jody will try it." He looked at Katrina. "You'll have some, won't you?" he encouraged.

Katrina tried to smile. "Yes, thank you."

Marissa reached over to take her hand. "I think we should try to contact our other GlobalFriends."

"Maybe through the Web site," suggested Jody.

"That's a good idea," Marissa agreed. "Or through e-mail letters. So we get their answers right away."

"There's no time to lose. An' our GlobalFriends are really good at comin' up with ideas and solutions to problems. I'd bet they could figure out who's takin' your costumes!" Jody exclaimed.

"Wait!" Marissa's father interrupted. "What are you talking about?"

"Whenever there's a problem or a mystery to be solved, the GlobalFriends Club is a good place to start. You can e-mail your pen pals to get lots of ideas. Kids from other countries sometimes look at problems differently," Marissa explained.

"And you can put a message on the board at the GlobalFriends Web site. Anybody in the Club can send a message back to you." Jody was excited.

"You'll need a computer," Marissa's father pointed out.

"Our father works for the government," Alexandria said. "We might use one of their computers. I will telephone him."

As Alexandria went in search of a telephone, Marissa asked her father for paper and a pen. "What shall we write?" she asked.

SEVEN

Jody quickly typed the message into the computer for the worldwide Web site board. Marissa and Jody had already sent e-mail letters to all of their GlobalFriends. Jody had barely finished typing when a message popped on the computer screen saying that there was an e-mail letter for Marissa.

Dear Marissa,

How terrible! There was a thief in our school last year. He, too, was stealing things from school lockers.

It was not easy to catch him because he was a janitor at the school. He was stealing things at night after everyone had gone home.

We finally caught him by setting a trap.

He seemed most interested in radios and calculators. Sometimes he would steal school books. So we loaded a locker with all the things he liked to steal. Then several of us hid in the locker area. We caught him red-handed! Maybe you could set a trap, too!

Your GlobalFriend from Spain, Carlotta

"Our thief might be one of the construction workers." Jody was thinking out loud.

"Perhaps." Katrina was doubtful.

"I really like her idea of setting a trap," Marissa announced. "We could do that with another costume. Wait! There's a letter coming in!"

Dear Jody,

Last year we thought someone stole all of our samba school costumes right before Carnival.

Remember, I wrote to you about the huge street parade that is a major part of the Carnival celebration. Only a few samba schools are chosen to compete. Ours was one of the schools selected.

Another school just outside our neighborhood was not chosen for the parade. So we thought they had stolen our costumes to prevent us from dancing in the parade. But, we found out that a relative of one of our girls had taken the costumes to be cleaned. We got them back and won the competition!

Maybe someone has taken your GlobalFriend's costumes for cleaning or repair.

Good luck in finding it!

Your GlobalFriend from Brazil, Selina

"I'll check with the Head Costumer in the morning," Katrina said,

reading the letter on the computer screen. "But I don't think she would have taken them without telling me. Look! There is another letter," Katrina pointed out. Jody quickly brought the new letter up on the screen.

>Dear Jody,
>   I am so sorry to hear of Katrina's misfortune.
>   How big are the lockers? If they are large enough for a person to fit into, maybe someone could hide inside the locker? In this way, we discovered how many of the Incan treasures were disappearing. Guards hid inside the actual gravesites.
>   Or you might just put a lock on the locker.
>   Your GlobalFriend from Peru, Menta

"Locks are not allowed on the lockers," Katrina explained. "It is forbidden."

"Well, I guess that's out," Marissa announced.

"Is your locker big enough for a person to hide inside?" Jody asked.

"Only if it is a very small person," Katrina said slowly.

"Look! There's another letter!" cried Marissa.

>Dear Marissa,
>   Have you tried following any of the suspects? There must be somebody that you think is stealing the costumes. Follow them!
>   Maybe they will try to steal something else.
>   If you can catch them stealing, you will have a much better case for the police.
>   Your GlobalFriend from Ireland, Kitty

"The police!" Katrina was chewing on her lip.

"Yes," Marissa said. "We really should report the theft to the authorities." She leaned over to read Kitty's letter again. "Does anybody think that it might be that instructor? You know, the one who yelled at you?"

"I forgot about him!" Jody exclaimed. "You're right! It might be him!"

"Professor Scalenski? It cannot be him!" Katrina protested.

"It has to be somebody," Marissa pointed out.

"It may not matter who the thief is," Katrina said sadly. "The Winter Fest performance is now only three days away. And I have no costume."

EIGHT

Jody's ice blue leotard fit Katrina perfectly. It even had long sleeves and a high neck like her first costume had! With sequins, feathers and maybe a few bows, it would be ideal!

"My mother gave me this two years ago." Jody was holding out a knit top covered with blue sequins. "She won't mind if we take it apart for a Winter Fest costume. It's a little small now, anyway. And I brought this, too." She shook out a sweater that was covered with ribbon bows of all colors.

"Yes!" cried Marissa, taking the sweater to see how the bows were attached. "This... And the sequins... And those feathers..." Marissa concentrated on showmanship, almost seeing in her mind how the costume would look under the circus spotlights. She eyed the white feather boa lying on the hotel bed. "We can make a great costume!"

Katrina was stretching in the leotard to make sure she could do all of her acrobatic moves in it. She straightened. "I do not know how to sew," she said hesitantly.

"I do," Marissa said matter-of-factly.

"Marissa got an A+ in sewin' class at school!" Jody burst out. She was proud of her best friend.

Marissa was eying the leotard on Katrina. "Yes," she said thoughtfully. "White feathers around the neckline. Different colored bows down both sleeves. And sequins over the entire body. It's going to be totally awesome!"

Katrina slipped into the bathroom to change out of the leotard and back into her street clothes. She came out moments later to find the other two girls deep in conversation.

"I still think Olga might be the thief," Marissa insisted. "Remember when Katrina was showing me that cartwheel to handstand move? Olga and her friends had just come out of the locker area."

"Maybe it was that mean instructor who yelled at Katrina," Jody suggested.

"It could not have been Professor Scalenski," Katrina said quietly. "He was just upset because we were talking so loudly, and he was right. Perhaps the noise was disturbing to students in the performance rings."

Marissa was busy snipping sequins off Jody's blue knit top. "Who do you think it is?" she asked Katrina.

"I do not think it was someone at the school. Certainly not a teacher. And not a classmate either." Puzzling all the while, Katrina slipped the elastic band off the end of her braid, then refastened it. "Perhaps it is one of the workmen. It is the only thing that makes

sense to me. Perhaps he doesn't know that the costumes are for the Winter Fest performance. He may not know how valuable they are."

"I think we ought to set a trap for the thief," Marissa stated, biting off a thread. "I think it's the only way we're going to catch him." She thought about it. "Or her," she added meaningfully.

"We should definitely set a trap," Jody agreed. "But not with this costume."

"No, not with this costume!" Katrina exclaimed.

"Now what have we got to make a fake costume with?" Jody wondered out loud, glancing around the hotel room. "I brought a couple of extra leotards."

"And we'll have plenty of feathers left over." Marissa held out most of the white boa. "And some sequins."

"I like this plan," Jody decided. "We'll leave the fake costume on the bench in front of Katrina's locker. One of us can hide inside the locker, and we'll catch 'em red-handed!"

NINE

"I'll hide inside the locker," Jody announced.

Katrina eyed her doubtfully. "You may be too tall."

"I could bend over." Jody demonstrated.

Katrina shook her head. "The locker has no room to bend. Even if it did, you could not bend like that for hours at a time."

Marissa glanced up from her sewing. "She's right. You would look like a pretzel. I'm not nearly as tall. Maybe I could do it."

There was a knock at the hotel room door. "I have wonderful news!!!" Alexandria stepped into the room, beaming.

Marissa snatched her loose sequins seconds before Alexandria bounced on the bed. "Careful," she warned.

"I'm sorry," Alexandria apologized. "But I really do have wonderful news!!!"

Jody and Marissa both laughed. Even Katrina smiled. "What is it, Alex?" she asked.

Alexandria was silent for three seconds, thinking. "No," she finally announced. "This is, to use your expression, *too cool*! You'll have to

guess." She plopped on the other bed, grinning from ear to ear.

"You found the costumes," Jody guessed.

Alexandria's face clouded. "Well, no. That would be really wonderful, too. But, no, I didn't find them. Guess again."

"Does it have to do with the Winter Fest?" asked Marissa, biting off a thread.

"Yes!" announced Alexandria.

"And does it have to do with the circus?" Marissa continued, thinking.

"Yes!"

"Is it about Katrina?" Marissa asked, knotting a length of thread and pulling it tight.

Alexandria shook her head. "No."

Marissa's head jerked up. "It's not?" she quizzed, really puzzled now.

Alexandria was still shaking her head, smiling. "No."

"If it's really cool, and it's not about Katrina, I have no idea," Marissa announced, giving up.

"Is it about the animals?" Katrina knew how much Alexandria loved the circus animals.

"Yes," Alexandria said with a sly smile.

"Is it the seals?" Katrina thought she had it figured out.

Alexandria shook her head with another sly grin. "Close. But no, it's not about the seals." She looked around the hotel room, waiting for more guesses. None came. "Come on, Jody. Have you got any ideas?" she coaxed.

Jody shook her head. "Not if it's not about the seals. Tell us."

Alexandria leaned back on the bed, grinning triumphantly. "Are you ready?" She looked from face to face. "You almost got it. It *is* about the animals. But not the seals. It's about the Mogodon circus animals. The tigers! One of the female tigers is pregnant! And she's going to have her babies any day! Maybe even while you're here! Real baby tiger cubs! Isn't that wonderful!!!"

Excited questions filled the small hotel room.

"Are you sure?"

"When?"

"She's really pregnant?"

"Who told you?"

Alexandria held up her hands, laughing. "One at a time! Yes, she's really pregnant. Yes, she's really going to give birth any day. And one of the Mogodon animal handlers told me. He said they're taking her out of the Winter Fest performance because she's so close. They don't want the excitement or anything to upset her. Isn't it great?!!" She looked around the hotel room again, seeing the feathers, sequins and bows for the first time. "What are you doing?"

Marissa explained their plan of making a show costume for Katrina.

Then Jody explained the idea of making a second costume for a trap.

"That's a good idea," Alexandria agreed. "But who's going to hide inside the locker?"

"We haven't decided yet." Marissa was sewing the feather boa around the leotard neckline.

"I could do it," Alexandria suggested.

Katrina shook her head again. "You are too tall, like Jody. It is my locker and my costumes. I should do it."

"You're too busy. And you've got classes all day long," Marissa pointed out. "I always knew being short was going to come in handy someday. I'll do it!"

Katrina was looking at Marissa. "Perhaps."

"What are you going to do when you catch the thief?" Alexandria asked. "What if it's Professor Scalenski? He's much bigger than you are."

"We could all just sorta be in the locker area. You know, for back up," Jody offered.

"No thief is going to try to steal something if he knows he's going to get caught," Marissa pointed out. "I'll just stay hidden inside the locker and watch to see who it is. I'm not going to leap out after him or try to catch him or anything. I'm just going to watch."

"Well, I think Kitty, your GlobalFriend from Ireland, had the right idea," Jody decided. "I'm gonna follow that mean instructor."

"We'll both follow him!" Alexandria bounced up from the bed, heading for the door. "I, too, think he may be taking the costumes!"

TEN

Decorated for Winter Fest, Moscow was just as beautiful during the day as it was at night. Following Professor Scalenski, Jody and Alexandria disappeared into a crowd of people crossing Red Square.

Jody nudged Alexandria. "What's that?"

Alexandria glanced off to the left. Over a dozen huge pieces of ice were standing in the square. "The ice will be carved into sculptures for Winter Fest. The sculptors will start tomorrow. It is a contest," she explained.

"Wow," murmured Jody. "Can we see 'em before we go back home?"

"Of course. The ice sculptures are for everyone to enjoy. Look, there he goes!" Alexandria pointed to Professor Scalenski who was hurrying down a side street.

The two friends split off from the crowd in the square. Luckily, Professor Scalenski never looked around. He simply hurried straight ahead.

"Have you ever been down this street before?" Jody whispered.

Tall, modern buildings rose straight up around a few very old buildings. They were just now passing an old building that looked like a church.

"A few times," Alexandria said quietly. "For the most part, these buildings are for doctors and dentists. People in the medical trade," she explained.

Professor Scalenski hurried into a modern building. Alexandria and Jody dashed through the door just as the professor disappeared into an elevator. Watching the dial above the elevator doors, they saw that the elevator stopped on the fourteenth floor. Alexandria stepped over to the building directory.

"The fourteenth floor is all doctors." She was scanning the directory. "*All* doctors." She looked around the building lobby. "We will wait."

Twenty-five minutes later, the professor came out of the elevator, heading for the lobby doors. Jody and Alexandria followed.

On the street again, he glanced at his watch, then walked even faster, disappearing into a building through a set of double doors.

"Where's he goin'?" Jody was trying not to pant.

"The underground Metro system," Alexandria guessed. "Hurry."

"The subway?" Jody was trying to remember all the horror stories she had ever heard about subways in America as they dashed through the doors. Once inside, she almost stopped dead in her tracks. "This is totally awesome!" she exclaimed in amazement, staring at the domed ceiling, chandeliers, archways and intricate moldings.

"We think it is one of the best subway systems in the world," agreed Alexandria as they dashed toward the open doors of the subway train, one car behind Professor Scalenski. "You can go anywhere in Moscow on the Metro."

Professor Scalenski left the train in a neighborhood of apartment buildings. Alexandria and Jody followed him to one of the buildings where, once again, he disappeared.

"Do you think he lives here?" Jody whispered.

Alexandria nodded. "It is very possible."

"What do we do now?" asked Jody.

Shrugging, Alexandria said, "We wait."

Ten long minutes later, Alexandria finally brought up what she'd been thinking about for days. "What would you think if I joined the GlobalFriends Club?"

"I think you'd really like it!" Jody and Alexandria were perched on the stoop outside Professor Scalenski's apartment building.

"So you don't think it is a stupid idea?" Alexandria turned to Jody, looking at her seriously.

"Nope!"

"You see," Alexandria explained. "I would really like to know a great many people in different countries. It's just that... Well, I don't know what I would talk to any of my GlobalFriends about."

Jody pointed to a banner across the street. It announced the Winter Fest. "You could talk about festivals and celebrations. Things that you are doin' at the circus school. Your classes. You could write to everybody about your travels and friends."

"That's right! I could write about meeting you and Marissa!" Smiling, Alexandria glanced inside the apartment building. The next moment, Alexandria was pushing Jody off the stoop. "Jump!" she whispered.

Alexandria and Jody jumped down the side of the stoop just as Professor Scalenski walked out the door. They followed him for three blocks to a small dressmaker's shop.

Staring in through the windows, they saw the professor examining what was clearly a girl's acrobatic costume.

"Is it one of Katrina's?" Jody whispered.

"I cannot be sure, but... I do not think so." Alexandria shook her head as Professor Scalenski was speaking to the shopkeeper. "Wait! He is coming now!" The two girls turned and walked rapidly down the street, away from the dressmaker's shop.

"Girls!" Professor Scalenski shouted. "You there! Girls!"

Without stopping, Jody and Alexandria looked at each other. Then Alexandria stopped. "He is an instructor at my school," she explained in a whisper. "I must listen to him." Jody stopped, too. They walked

back to the professor standing on the snow-covered sidewalk.

"Why are you following me?" Professor Scalenski demanded suddenly.

Taken by surprise, Alexandria was speechless. Jody was thinking fast. "Gosh, sir," she said quickly. "We knew you were sick, but we didn't think you were that sick!"

Professor Scalenski frowned. "I am not ill. What makes you think that I am ill?"

"You went right from school to a doctor's office," Jody explained. "Why would you see a doctor if you weren't sick?"

Professor Scalenski clasped his hands behind his back, staring from Jody to Alexandria, then back to Jody. "The doctor was not for me," he finally said. "He is my daughter's doctor." Professor Scalenski sighed. "Lena also attends the circus school. Three weeks ago, she fell from the low wire and sprained her ankle. She has been

48

unable to practice. Still, she was selected for our show at the Winter Fest. I was talking with her doctor to make sure that a performance now will not injure her further."

"I heard about that!" Alexandria exclaimed. "I did not know that Lena was your daughter, sir."

"Yes, she is my daughter." Professor Scalenski was staring at Jody. "It is good that we meet like this. I would like to apologize for my temper display in the locker area earlier this week. Perhaps you will understand when I tell you that Lena fell from the low wire when she was startled by an unexpected noise. I am sorry. I was wrong. It is important that circus performers learn to expect the unexpected."

Jody looked at Alexandria and Alexandria looked at Jody. Feeling embarrassed, Alexandria mumbled, "It is we who are sorry, Professor Scalenski." She explained about Katrina's missing costumes, even admitting that they thought the professor might be taking them.

"No, I am not your thief," Professor Scalenski said, smiling. "But I will notify the school authorities. We will catch the person who is responsible."

Walking back to the hotel from the Metro station, Jody kicked a pile of snow into the street. "Well, the thief is definitely not Professor Scalenski."

Alexandria shook her head. "No, definitely not."

"But who is it?" Jody wondered out loud. "Who in the blue blazes is it?"

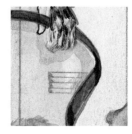

ELEVEN

Marissa bent her knees just a little. The coat hook inside the locker was digging into the top of her head. Turning just a little, she could see the fake costume laying on the bench in front of Katrina's locker. Standing on one leg, she stretched the other leg out the crack in the slightly open locker door. But before she could get the kinks out of her muscles, she heard voices. Silently, she drew her leg back into the locker.

At first, the girlish voices were just a mumble jumble of Russian. Then one girl spoke louder. "We agreed to speak English. It is good practice."

The other girls groaned. The girl spoke even louder. "An agreement is an agreement! If we cannot speak their language, how can we communicate with the Americans? I wish to know many of their acrobatic moves. How else can we learn from them?"

Another girl interrupted. "Perhaps they should be learning from us!"

"We should all be learning from each other," the first girl said. She

50

walked in front of the bench, and Marissa could see that it was Olga. She stopped, staring down at the bench. "Who does this costume belong to?"

Marissa could see the other four girls shaking their heads. "It should be put away in a locker," one of the girls said. "This is not a proper place for it."

"Since we don't know who it belongs to, we should not touch it. Leave it there." Olga walked past the locker on her way to the dressing room. "I wish that I could do a handspring on the low wire the way Katrina does it. I think that I am going to ask her to help me." The voices faded as the girls walked through the door.

Scrunching her mouth, Marissa was thinking hard inside the locker. It sure didn't sound like Olga was the thief!

Suddenly, Marissa could hear a loud voice announcing something in Russian. Then the door to the performance arena banged open. A dozen monkeys were being brought through the locker area. They had leashes attached to their collars, and there were two monkeys to each handler.

As Marissa peeked through the slightly open locker door, one of the monkeys twisted out of his collar. Quick as lightening, he leaped to the top of the row of lockers, then jumped to the overhead light.

Swinging back and forth, he was chattering loudly, screeching almost. Scrambling, one of the handlers gave his leashes to another handler, then he climbed on top of the lockers as well. Walking carefully and holding out his hands, he approached the monkey. At the

51

very last moment, the monkey grinned and leaped over the handler's head.

Marissa could see another handler handing off his leashes to join the handler on top of the lockers. Now there were two handlers and a monkey on top of the lockers, and more handlers with the rest of the monkeys on the floor.

As Marissa watched, the monkeys on the floor started jumping and racing around each other, tangling their leashes into a knotted mess. The monkey on top of the lockers had leaped up to another overhead light and was swinging back and forth, screeching again. Marissa had to shove a hand into her mouth to keep from laughing out loud.

Fifteen minutes later, the loose monkey was finally recaptured. The leashes were sorted out enough to separate the monkeys. Holding the monkeys in their arms, the disgruntled handlers left the locker area, and Marissa could finally laugh.

Her laughter was short lived. The same loud Russian voice as before was announcing something again. Marissa swallowed her laugh and crouched back into the locker.

She heard a whip crack. Peeking around the open door, her eyes grew wide with fright. The tigers were coming through! Marissa drew back as far as she could and swung the door shut, latching the door on the inside. Now she was safe inside the locker with the door closed. But she couldn't see the costume!

Standing on her tiptoes, Marissa could just barely see out the slats in the metal door. Luckily, she could pretty much see straight down,

and the fake costume was still there on the bench.

The whip cracked again. Marissa could see one giant orange and black-striped paw pad by the bench. A tiger tail brushed the costume. Then Marissa saw another tiger walk by, his huge furry paws silent on the floor. He sniffed the costume, then walked on.

The last tiger was well behind the first two. It looked to Marissa as though this last tiger might be fatter. She was certainly slower.

The whip cracked again, and the tiger handler called out the tiger's name, coaxing her forward.

The tiger barely looked up. She was sniffing the fake costume laying on the bench. Marissa could see her two front paws and her head, neck and shoulders. She looked very strong! And very big! Her nose was wet. It was leaving wet spots on the leotard. Then, quick as a flash, the tiger snatched up the fake costume in her mouth! Dashing after the other tigers, she raced out of the locker room!

TWELVE

"It was the mother tiger who was stealing my costumes all along," Katrina explained, smiling. She was twisting her thick red braid into a knot on the back of her head. "Nobody noticed because she carried them inside her mouth. She was making a bed in her sleeping box. You know, inside her cage. The tiger animal handler thinks it was because of the baby tigers. She wants them to have a nice bed when they are born. He says that they do that out in the wild, too. They gather dried plants and grasses to make a bed."

"Are your costumes okay?" Jody asked.

Katrina laughed. "Oh, no. They are shredded now. She has ripped them to pieces. The animal handler took them away. He was concerned that the sequins and beads might be harmful to the babies. He gave her some towels to make a bed instead."

"You mean all your beautiful costumes are gone!" Jody exclaimed.

"But I have this beautiful costume to wear!" Katrina said proudly. She was wearing the costume that Marissa had made for her.

And she was right! The costume was beautiful! In the bright

lights of the dressing room at the Winter Fest stage, the blue sequins sparkled. The colored bows on the sleeves shimmered. And the white feathers around the neckline floated softly, framing her face.

A woman came into the dressing room, speaking in Russian to Katrina. Katrina turned to her friends. "I am sorry. I will have to leave now. It is time to warm up for my performance. You may want to explore the Winter Fest. There are many acts being performed on this stage. And you should see the ice sculptures. There are skating performances on the ice rink. Women and men and ice-dancing couples."

"Dad said that he would take us for a horse-drawn sleigh ride, too!" Marissa cried, excited.

Katrina laughed. "You might find a sleigh pulled by reindeer as well."

"Real reindeer!" Jody was amazed. "Pullin' sleighs!"

"Real reindeer," Katrina assured her. "But be sure to come back in time for my performance. It will be two hours from now."

* * *

"This is so cool!" Jody exclaimed as she pulled on her mittens.

Marissa opened the door, and they stepped out into the snowy cold of Russia's Winter Fest. Crowds of people were hurrying from one performance to another. There was so much to see and do! And everyone was laughing and talking gaily. Clouds of steam from their breath hung frostily in the air.

Alexandria and Marissa's father walked toward them, carrying

mugs of hot, milky tea. Enough for all four of them.

"You've got to see the ice sculptures!" Alexandria insisted. "This year they are the best I have ever seen!"

"The skaters are incredible!" Marissa's father said, draping an arm around Marissa's shoulders and hugging her. "And the desk clerk at the hotel told me how to get to the ski hills and toboggan runs. You know, a lot of the kids performing here at the Winter Fest are hoping to be in the Olympics one day. They're that good!"

* * *

Inside the auditorium, the audience lights came down slowly as the lights on the circus ring came up.

The circus master in his sparkling white sequin coat stepped up to the microphone. "Ladies and gentlemen..." he said in both Russian and English. "Children of all ages... Welcome one and all!"

Jody and Marissa stared wide-eyed as students from the Moscow

58

Circus School took the stage. Spellbound, they watched act after act. Acrobats! Tumblers! Clowns! Seals and dogs!

And horses! Boys and girls leaping from the ground to stand on the backs of galloping horses. Doing handstands on horseback.

And the trapeze! Flying through the air. Swinging from the trapeze bar to a partner's hands and back to the trapeze bar again. Twists and turns and somersaults in the air.

And more acrobats! Human pyramids. Circus students climbing thirty feet in the air on the backs and shoulders of more students. And the tightwire...! As Marissa and Jody gazed, mesmerized, Katrina dashed onto the stage. Flipping over and over in a series of cartwheels, she landed next to a tightly stretched rope that led to the tightwire strung twenty feet above the floor. Her shimmering blue show costume sparkled in the spotlight.

In a flash, she climbed the rope, hand over hand, to the tightwire. The drumroll echoed as she saluted the audience from the tightwire platform.

Holding her arms straight out for balance, Katrina stepped onto the tightwire. Confidently, never missing a beat, she walked to the middle. Then dropped to a crouch. Rolling forward, she clasped her hands around the wire, bringing both feet straight up into the air in a handstand. Swinging backward, Katrina spun around the wire, again coming to a stop in a handstand. Lowering her legs, she balanced on the wire, standing straight. Slowly, standing on one leg alone, she lifted the other leg straight in the air above her head. The audience gasped.

Lowering her leg, Katrina danced across the wire. Almost reaching the platform on the far side, she bent forward and flipped over completely in a cartwheel that ended on the platform. Applause thundered as the audience roared.

Smiling, Katrina found Marissa and Jody in the audience. Her arms outstretched, she mouthed, "Thank you." And blew them a kiss.

* * *

As they walked backstage to congratulate Katrina, Alexandria stepped up beside Marissa. "Marissa? I think I'd like to join the GlobalFriends Club."

Jody turned around from where she was walking ahead of them with Marissa's father. "You're really gonna love it! Different countries are a blast!"

"And different people. And learning different things," Alexandria pointed out.

"Yes, like learning how to trust," Marissa said quietly. "Learning to trust others and how to be trustworthy yourself is the most important lesson Russia taught me. I'm never going to forget it."

Welcome to
Global ❤ Friends
A D V E N T U R E S

Learn about the sights, cultures and people of global countries throughthis thrilling adventure series. The kids in the GlobalFriends Club use their communication skills through letters and the GlobalFriends Chat room (on the web site globalfriends.com) to solve every mystery. Full color illustrations. 64 pages.

The GlobalFriends Adventures are just the beginning. GlobalFriends is an adventurous collection of global dolls, accessories, videos, newsletters and more! If you or a friend would like to receive a GlobalFriends catalog, please mail in this page to: GlobalFriends 333 Hatch Drive, San Mateo, CA 94404-1162. A GlobalFriends catalog will be in your mail box very soon!

- -

Yes! Please send me a GlobalFriends catalog!

Name: _____

Address: _____

City: _____ State: _____ Zip: _____

My Birthday is: _____

My age is: _____

Parent's Signature: _____

More GlobalFriends Adventures™ books are available through GlobalFriends™ catalog.

The Haunted English Riding Stable

The Secret Egyptian Code

The Lost Treasure of the Rain Forest